KID DYNOBITE

—— MADELINE SUNSHINE ——

P9-ELG-967

SCHOLASTIC BOOK SERVICES
New York Toronto London Auckland Sydney Tokyo

Illustrated by Gordon Kibbee

This book is from Sprint Starter Library A.
Other books in this library are:
Our Park
The Power
The Weeping Ghost
Mr. Marvel

Copyright © 1978 by Madeline Sunshine. All rights reserved. Published by Scholastic Book Services, a division of Scholastic Magazines, Inc.

12 11 10 9 8 7 6 5 4 3 2 1   9   8 9/7 0 1 2 3/8

On a planet far from Earth lived a very special boy. He could fly. He could lift big buildings with his teeth. He could even walk on his nose. His name was KID DYNOBITE.

"Kid," said Pop Dynobite. "You are needed on Earth. You must leave at once. There are people to save. There are wrongs to right. And there are great ball games on TV."

5

"But how will I get there?" asked the boy.

"In a flying machine," said Mom Dynobite. "Pop and I made it last night."

"All right," said Kid Dynobite. "I'll go. But do I have to wear these braces on my teeth? They look silly!"

"Silly?" exclaimed his mother. "You should feel lucky! Superboy had to walk around in blue tights."

"Besides," said his father. "Those braces give you your special powers. Without them, you would not be KID DYNOBITE!"

So, boy and braces climbed into the flying machine.

"Kid," said his mother. "To use your powers on Earth, snap your teeth together three times. And," she added, "stay away from bubble gum!"

With that, the take-off began. Five...four...three...two....

"Wait!" screamed Kid Dynobite. "I just remembered! I don't know how to fly this thing!"

But it was too late. He was already shooting through the sky.

WILL THE KID GET TO EARTH SAFELY?
WILL HE BE ABLE TO STAY AWAY FROM BUBBLE GUM?

Things looked bad for Kid Dynobite. He had no idea how to fly the flying machine. But then suddenly he heard a strange voice.

"I am 006, your Flying Machine. Do not worry. I fly myself. We will reach Earth at

10:00 P.M. Sit back and enjoy the ride."

Sure enough, at exactly 10:00 they landed. Kid Dynobite got out of the flying machine. It was dark. Something strange was headed in his direction.

"An Earth creature," he thought.

Just then, he heard a loud noise. The flying machine was taking off.

"Where are you going?" cried the boy.

"Home," said the machine. "Your parents need me."

"But what about me?" screamed Kid Dynobite.

"You have super powers," said the machine. "Good luck!" Then it disappeared.

Kid Dynobite turned around. The Earth creature was still headed toward him.

"I don't believe it!" he said. "Earth creatures have metal bodies. And their eyes are made of glass. And they light up!"

Suddenly the creature made a strange sound.

"That does not sound friendly," thought Kid Dynobite. "I had better call on my special powers."

He began to snap his teeth together. But, before he could finish, his braces locked.

"Oh, no!" he thought. "Now I can't snap three times! What am I going to do?"

The Earth creature was getting closer and closer. It kept making the same scary sound.

WILL KID DYNOBITE BE ABLE TO CALL ON HIS SPECIAL POWERS?

WILL THE EARTH CREATURE BE FRIENDLY?

11

Kid Dynobite faced the Earth creature.

"Say!" yelled a voice. "What are you doing? This road is for cars only."

"Of course," thought Kid Dynobite. "That's not a creature. It's a car!"

The car pulled over and two people got out.

"Are you all right?" asked the woman.
Kid Dynobite could not answer.

"Look, Harry," the woman said. "His braces have locked. That's why he can't speak."

Kid Dynobite was lucky. Harry was a dentist. He fixed his braces in no time.

"Thank you," said the boy. "Now I can use my special powers again."

"Special powers!" exclaimed Harry and Martha.

Kid Dynobite tried to explain. But Harry and Martha had a hard time believing him. Finally Harry turned to his wife.

"I think this boy is a little whacky!" he whispered. "Let's just get him home."

Ten minutes later they were inside Harry and Martha's house.

"Now I'll show you my special powers," said Kid Dynobite.

He snapped his teeth together three times. Suddenly he was flying around the room. With one hand, he picked up the couch. Harry and Martha screamed. They were sitting on it.

"Put us down!" they cried. "Please, put us down!"

But Kid Dynobite was not listening. He was too busy showing off his special powers. Just then, a policeman came by.

"What is going on in there?" he yelled. "Open up or I'll break the door down!"

WILL THE KID STOP FLYING AROUND?
WILL THE POLICEMAN BREAK THE DOOR DOWN?

CHAPTER 4

The policeman's voice brought Kid Dynobite back to Earth. He placed the couch back on the floor. Then Harry called out:

"It's all right, Officer. We were just playing — myself, the wife, and our son."

And that's how it happened. Harry, Martha,

and Kid Dynobite became a family. They gave
him a new name—Elroy Frankfurter. Elroy was
Harry's father's name. Frankfurter was
Martha's favorite food. It was also their last
name. The next day, Harry and Martha took
Elroy to school.

"Son," said Harry. "Don't ever tell anyone about your powers."

"But, Harry...I mean, Dad," said Elroy. "I was sent to Earth to use my powers!"

"Only when there is real danger," said Harry. "At other times they must be kept a secret."

Elroy's school days were no fun. He tried to make friends. He tried to save people. But no one needed saving. The other children laughed at him.

"Say, metal mouth," yelled one boy.

"Look at the size of those braces!" yelled another.

"Stop it! Stop laughing at me!" cried Elroy. "Or...or I'll throw you all into the ocean!"

"Did you hear that? He is going to throw us into the ocean!"

"He can't," said a boy named Jack. "He can't get that close to water. His braces will rust!"

The other children laughed even harder.

"All right," said Elroy. "You asked for it!"

With that, he began to snap his teeth together. Once...twice....

WILL KID DYNOBITE SNAP HIS TEETH THE THIRD TIME?

WILL HE THROW THE LAUGHING CHILDREN INTO THE OCEAN?

19

Elroy "KID DYNOBITE" Frankfurter began to
snap his teeth a third time. But then....

"NO!" he said to himself. "I can't do it. I'm a
good guy. Good guys right wrongs. They save
those in danger. They watch ball games on TV.

20

But throwing people into the ocean — no way!"

He carefully closed his mouth. Then he looked around. The other children were still laughing and joking. They didn't know what a close call they had had.

Just then Elroy heard one of them say:

"The fair is in town today. Let's all go!"

"What is a fair?" asked Elroy.

"It's a place where you play games and win prizes," explained a boy named Paul. "And it has scary rides that fly through the air."

"Those rides sound dangerous!" exclaimed Elroy.

"They are," said Paul.

And that's what made up Elroy's mind. He was going to the fair.

When they got there, the first stop was the fun house. Next, they decided to go on the rides. Just then, Elroy saw Paul put something into his mouth.

"What is that?" he asked.

"Here, have some," said Paul. "It's good."

Elroy took a piece.

"Chew it," said Paul. "You are supposed to chew it."

Elroy bit down. "It is good," he said. "What is it called?"

"Don't you know!" said Paul. "That's bubble gum."

"Bubble gum!" screamed Elroy. "Oh, no!"

WHAT WILL THE BUBBLE GUM DO TO ELROY?

WHAT WILL ELROY DO NOW?

Elroy tried to get the gum out of his braces. It was too late. His teeth were locked together.

"Hurry, Elroy," said Paul. "We want to go on the cable cars."

Elroy didn't answer.

"What is the matter?" said another boy. "Are you scared or something?"

Elroy still didn't answer.

"Forget it, metal mouth," said a third boy. "We are going without you." They left and got on the ride.

So Elroy was left all alone. Then suddenly, he heard loud screams. The cable holding up the cable cars was breaking. Children were trapped in the air.

"People in danger!" Elroy thought. "This is a job for KID DYNOBITE. What can I do? My braces are locked!"

Just then he had an idea. He ran around the fair grounds. He was looking for the strong man's tent. At last he found it. He dashed inside. He explained his problem as best he could. The strong man seemed to understand. He pulled and pulled on Elroy's mouth.

Finally, with a loud pop, Elroy's mouth flew open. The bubble gum flew out. It landed on the strong man's nose. Elroy thanked the strong man. Then he quickly ran toward the cable cars. As he ran, he snapped his teeth together once, then twice. The screams of the trapped children got louder and louder.

WILL ELROY BE IN TIME TO SAVE THE CHILDREN?

WILL THE CABLE CARS FALL DOWN?

Kid Dynobite snapped his teeth together the third time. In a flash, he was in the air. He flew toward the breaking cable. Just then, the people standing below noticed him.

"Look!" yelled a man. "Up in the sky! It's a

bird! It's a plane! It's a boy with braces?!"

"Yes," said a woman. "And he is wearing a strange T-shirt. It says, 'I save people. I turn wrongs to right. I'm the one, the only, KID DYNOBITE!'"

Meanwhile, Kid Dynobite reached the breaking cable. As he did, it began to snap. He grabbed both ends with his teeth. A man below started the cable cars again. Slowly they began to move. In a few minutes, each car had reached the ground. Everyone was safe. Then, his work done, Kid Dynobite quietly flew off. He landed right behind the strong man's tent. He changed out of his Kid Dynobite clothing. Then he raced off to join the others.

"Where were you?" asked Paul. "You missed everything!"

"That's right," said another boy. "We were almost killed!"

"But," added Paul. "We were saved by Kid Dynobite."

"Kid Dynobite?" said Elroy, trying not to smile.

"Yes," said Paul. "He is a boy, just like us. But he has these super braces."

"You know," said a third boy. "I wish I had braces like that."

Elroy didn't say a word. He just looked at the others and smiled.

WILL ELROY EVER LET ON THAT HE IS REALLY KID DYNOBITE?

WILL THE OTHER CHILDREN GET BRACES?

YOUR GUESS IS AS GOOD AS MINE!